The Magic Shell

BY NICHOLASA MOHR

ILLUSTRATIONS BY RUDY GUTIERREZ

Para Alba Moza

Happy Reading.

SCHOLASTIC INC.
New York

Library of Congress Cataloging-in-Publication Data

Mohr, Nicholasa.
The magic shell / Nicholasa Mohr.
p.   cm.
Summary: When his family moves from the Dominican Republic
to New York City, Jaime uses his uncle's
magical shell to call up happy memories.
ISBN 0-590-47110-4
[1. Emigration and immigration — Fiction.
2. Dominican Republic — Emigration and immigration — Fiction.
3. Moving, Household — Fiction. 4. Shells — Fiction.
5. New York (N.Y.) — Fiction.]
I. Title.
PZ7.M7276Jai   1995
[E] — dc20   93-30403
CIP
AC

12 11 10 9 8 7 6 5 4 3 2 1   5 6 7 8 9/9 0/0

Printed in the U.S.A.   37

First printing, September 1995

Designed by Marijka Kostiw

For my sons,

DAVID AND JASON MOHR,

with affection and joyous

memories of their

childhood

days.

N. M.

Thank you to

MARILYN BAEZ AND FAMILY

for showing me firsthand how beautiful the

Dominican people are.

R. G.

Contents

1

LEAVING HOME

"**OH, ROSA**, we'll miss you all so much . . ." Jaime's Aunt Carmen told his mother. Tears were streaming down her cheeks.

"We're going to miss all of you, too," answered his mom, hugging his Aunt Carmen, Aunt Diana, and Cousin Patricia. Everybody was hugging all at once and crying lots of tears.

Jaime made sure to dodge out of their way. He didn't enjoy getting wet kisses and hugs from all these crying ladies. This included his mom. The warm sun and cool mountain air made it a perfect December day.

"And we sure are going to miss our beautiful weather," sobbed his mom, wiping her nose.

His parents looked so unhappy that Jaime

Ramos hoped they might even change their minds about moving so far away from the Dominican Republic. At one o'clock this afternoon, their plane was leaving for New York City.

Jaime felt he was the most unhappy of them all. He knew he would miss his home and especially his best friends whom he had played with since he was a little kid. But he wasn't going to let everybody see him crying and acting silly.

He took one last look around the only home he had ever known. Everything was gone. The bare walls and the empty house made their voices echo.

Who had ever asked his opinion about moving? This made Jaime feel more angry than sad. It didn't seem right. His life was just fine the way it was and didn't need changes. It wasn't as though he hadn't argued and pleaded with his parents until he was purple in the face.

"Why can't we stay right here in our village? Why do we have to go live in the United States? I don't even know anybody there!"

"Jaime, I already told you . . . because I've got a great job over there with good benefits," his dad explained. "And I'll have opportunities for advancement. That's why!"

Jaime's father was an electrical engineer. Many people said that Pedro Ramos was one of the best electrical engineers in the northern province of the Dominican Republic.

Jaime's mother was no help, either. "It's all for the best," she said. "Once you get used to things in the United States you'll do just fine."

"You and Marietta will go to a splendid school," his dad had argued, "and besides, everything is already settled."

Jaime just got more and more angry. The word *settled* sounded so final and it made him feel powerless.

He couldn't even count on his little sister Marietta to take his side. She was busy smiling and saying silly things to Pepita, her favorite rag doll, and acting as if everything was still the same. But what did she know? She was only two years old and couldn't even talk sense yet.

Just then, his father's brother, Uncle Manuel, pulled up in his green Jeep to drive them to the airport in Puerto Plata.

All the neighbors and relatives had gathered around to help and to say their last good-byes. They began helping his father and uncle load the Jeep with all the suitcases and cartons that were piled outside their house. Jaime found his bicycle and brought it to his dad.

"I think we have room for my bike," he said.

"Jaime! You know we can't take your bike with us," snapped his dad. "We've agreed that Aunt Carmen will keep it for you until we return for a visit. Now, put it back!"

Jaime held back his tears. He sure would miss riding his bike around the mountain paths. His mom had already told him that there were no mountains in New York City. Jaime wanted to argue, but he did as he was told. Once his dad made up his mind there was no way to change it.

Jaime's best buddies, Wilfredo, Lucy and Sarita, were also waiting to say good-bye.

"Aren't you afraid to go up in an airplane?" Lucy asked.

"He's not scared," answered Wilfredo. "Right, Jaime?" Wilfredo was his best pal.

"That's right . . ." Jaime nodded. "I'm not scared at all." This was true. Jaime was *not* scared — in fact, he had always been curious about riding a plane.

"My cousin Santos went up in a plane," Sarita told them. "He said it felt just like you could be sitting in your living room. You didn't feel nothing . . ."

"Will you promise to write and tell us what it feels like?" asked Lucy.

"Sure, I will," Jaime promised, although he really wasn't thinking about the plane ride just then.

All his friends were standing around talking as if nothing had changed. But Jaime couldn't stop thinking about how, in a little while, he would be gone. He would be far away from his village, far away from Montaña Verde. His friends would still all be here. But he would be in a strange new place, with no one to play with. It felt scary to know that he was moving away for good.

He recalled how at sunrise this morning

when the first rooster began to crow, he had climbed on his bike and pedaled over to visit his great-uncle, Tío Ernesto. He knew he needed help and had gone to Tío Ernesto to get some good advice.

Tío Ernesto lived by himself farther up in the mountains.

Tío Ernesto had been a merchant seaman for many years and traveled the world over. He never married and had no children. When Tío Ernesto retired, he purchased a few acres of land in Montaña Verde, away from the village. He called his small homestead *mi paraíso*, my paradise, where he lived simply and happily. He grew vegetables and herbs in his garden and owned two goats, a few chickens and some geese.

Tío Ernesto became well known as a wise old man who had seen the whole world. Folks would travel up to his wooden cabin to seek his counsel about all kinds of problems. He'd prepare special teas for curing bad colds, fevers and headaches. And he made herbal remedies for depression, bad tempers and nasty behavior. Just last month Tío Ernesto had solved a terrible quarrel between two neighbors who refused to share the only path leading to the river. Both neighbors claimed it was their own private road. First Tío Ernesto sat them down and gave them each a glass of his herbal refreshment. Their bad tempers disappeared and soon they agreed that the road was big enough for everyone to use. Now they were good friends.

People spoke about his wonderful gift for spiritual healing. Some believed that Tío Ernesto possessed magical powers.

Early on the morning of his departure, Jaime had sat on the wooden stool watching Tío Ernesto as he prepared some tea. "Tío," he said, "I don't want to go to the United States. But my parents won't listen to me."

Jaime liked talking to his great-uncle because he always listened.

Tío Ernesto told him that he understood how sad Jaime must be feeling. That was why he was giving him a special present to take to New York City. Tío Ernesto reached inside his old sideboard and took out a box wrapped in brown paper and tied with twine. He held it in his large bony hands.

"This is for you," he said and gave it to Jaime.

When Jaime took the box he felt a slight movement. "What's inside?" he asked.

"It's a conch shell," replied Tío Ernesto.

"Is the conch still alive?" Jaime asked.

Tío Ernesto smiled and answered, "It is only the shell."

Jaime was confused and thought, *What kind*

11 I do with

ly, "all of

this shell.

Montaña

fort you."

ny fingers

He showed

to his ear.

trate and

aring sea

mories of

Montaña

n and the

box, Tío

ed him.

I the time

ally need

it is just

cked the

ve again.

his par-

ents had kept on u...
last-minute packi...
fast, Jaime had al...
only looked up fro...
he heard his name...
"Jaime . . . Jaim...
ing down the path...
"Jaime," he whi...
present?"
Jaime nodded s...
"Good," Tío ...
wisely."
After everyone...
and the Jeep wa...
their boxes, trun...
to go.
Jaime took one...
waved to his fri...
winding road. E...
iar slowly disa...
longer see his vil...
turned onto the...
to the airport in...

of gift is this? He asked, "What will I do with such a present, Tío?"

"Ah," Tío Ernesto nodded wisely, "all of your memories are stored inside this shell. When you become homesick for Montaña Verde, this special shell will comfort you." Tío Ernesto cupped his long skinny fingers as if he were holding the shell. He showed Jaime how to bring the shell close to his ear.

"You must be quiet and concentrate and listen carefully. You will hear the roaring sea and soon you will have your memories of home — of our mountain village, Montaña Verde, where the skies touch heaven and the earth smiles down at the sea."

When Jaime began to unwrap the box, Tío Ernesto put his hand out and stopped him.

"Not yet!" he told him. "Wait until the time is right. It works only when you really need it to help you remember. Otherwise it is just a useless old shell."

Later that morning, as Jaime packed the box inside his trunk, it seemed to move again. He was very tempted to open it, but his parents had kept on urging him to finish with his last-minute packing. Things were going so fast, Jaime had almost no time to think. He only looked up from his packing once, when he heard his name being called.

"Jaime . . . Jaime!" It was Tío Ernesto coming down the path to say his last farewells.

"Jaime," he whispered, "did you pack your present?"

Jaime nodded sadly.

"Good," Tío Ernesto smiled. "Use it wisely."

After everyone said their final good-byes and the Jeep was squeezed full with all of their boxes, trunks and suitcases, it was time to go.

Jaime took one last look at his house and waved to his friends as they drove down the winding road. Everything that was so familiar slowly disappeared. Soon he could no longer see his village. And then, Uncle Manuel turned onto the main highway and sped off to the airport in Puerto Plata.

*   *   *

his old sideboard and took out a box wrapped in brown paper and tied with twine. He held it in his large bony hands.

"This is for you," he said and gave it to Jaime.

When Jaime took the box he felt a slight movement. "What's inside?" he asked.

"It's a conch shell," replied Tío Ernesto.

"Is the conch still alive?" Jaime asked.

Tío Ernesto smiled and answered, "It is only the shell."

Jaime was confused and thought, *What kind*

nasty behavior. Just last month Tío Ernesto had solved a terrible quarrel between two neighbors who refused to share the only path leading to the river. Both neighbors claimed it was their own private road. First Tío Ernesto sat them down and gave them each a glass of his herbal refreshment. Their bad tempers disappeared and soon they agreed that the road was big enough for everyone to use. Now they were good friends.

People spoke about his wonderful gift for spiritual healing. Some believed that Tío Ernesto possessed magical powers.

Early on the morning of his departure, Jaime had sat on the wooden stool watching Tío Ernesto as he prepared some tea. "Tío," he said, "I don't want to go to the United States. But my parents won't listen to me."

Jaime liked talking to his great-uncle because he always listened.

Tío Ernesto told him that he understood how sad Jaime must be feeling. That was why he was giving him a special present to take to New York City. Tío Ernesto reached inside

Jaime sat in his window seat next to his dad and watched the airplane fill with people. Then the big motors roared and the plane moved along the runway. It sped faster and lifted off the ground. Jaime quickly reached out and grabbed his dad's arm.

"Don't worry, son. Everything is going to be okay. Soon we will be up in the clouds," said his dad as he squeezed Jaime's hand gently.

Jaime looked out the window and saw his beloved Dominican Republic get smaller, and then tiny, until it became a dot that disappeared into space. The plane continued flying through white clouds for what seemed like forever. Down below was the blue Caribbean Sea. Jaime felt as if he were in a dream. Sarita's cousin Santos was right; it did feel like he almost wasn't even moving.

Jaime thought about New York. *What kind of place was this United States? What were the kids like there? Would he like them? Would they like him? Would he make friends there?*

His thoughts were interrupted by the voice

of the flight attendant. "Fasten your seat belts, please. We will be landing at John F. Kennedy Airport in approximately ten minutes."

Jaime looked out the window. Tall skyscrapers and gray buildings outlined the horizon and stretched out as far as he could see. There was not a mountain in sight. And the clouds and the water were as gray as the buildings between them. What a strange place. Jaime sighed and swallowed as his stomach did a flip-flop.

2

A NEW HOME
IN NEW YORK CITY

IT WAS EARLY in December and New York City was braving a cold spell. The temperature outdoors was below freezing. When Jaime walked out of the airport to the taxi stand, a blast of ice-cold air left him breathless. His ears and cheeks stung, and his eyes began to tear. Jaime had never experienced this kind of cold back home, and it shocked his whole body.

The cold spell continued, and by the end of his first week, Jaime had only gone outdoors twice. That was to shop with his mom. Each time, the cold had made his nose run, and he shivered all over.

Everyone in the family had caught bad colds. Their new apartment echoed with sneezing and coughing.

"We all have to stay inside until we get well again," declared his mother. Only his dad left every morning to go to work. Jaime wanted no part of the horrible frigid weather outside. He thought, *At least it's warm indoors*, and he decided not to bother his mother about going outside.

Every morning Jaime would look out of the large picture window in his new bedroom. He was high up above the ground on the sixteenth floor. Instead of mountains, Jaime could see endless rows of high buildings. It gave him a weird feeling to be living way up in the air.

Off in the distance he saw a long bridge. A river ran underneath it, with boats traveling up and down. His dad said it was called the East River. On one side was Manhattan, and on the other side was the borough of Queens where they lived. The water that flowed beneath the bridge was muddy brown instead of a clear bright blue like the Caribbean Sea. The streets were crowded with traffic. The loud sounds of trucks rumbling, cars honking and fire engines screaming

echoed all the way up into Jaime's bedroom. *Was it always so noisy?* he wondered. Down below the people scurried around in all directions. They looked like busy bugs.

Jaime missed the quiet of the mountains and the trees of Montaña Verde. Most of all he missed the freedom to step out of his own front door and play outside. Instead he felt locked up in this huge building. He yearned to be out under the warm sun playing with Wilfredo, Lucy and Sarita.

Jaime did like watching television. They had a lot more TV stations here than they did back home. But everyone spoke in English. He did not understand what they were saying and he soon became bored. Occasionally, Jaime tried the Spanish TV stations. They mostly showed soap operas or musical numbers. He found those stations plain dull. There was just not much to do in his new home.

Jaime did think the elevator in their building was really neat, though. He liked riding up and down with his mom. One morning, he quietly left his apartment and pressed the button for the elevator and waited. When the doors opened, he stepped inside and pushed all the buttons until every floor was lit up. Then he rode up and down and up and down — having a grand time!

As people walked in and out of the elevator, they smiled at him in a friendly way.

"Are you the new elevator man?" asked a middle-aged man with gray hair. He gave Jaime a big smile. Jaime didn't understand what the man said, but he nodded and smiled back anyway.

When Jaime saw a couple of boys about his own age, he wanted to say something. The boys were all bundled up in coats and scarfs and were carrying school bags. He was curious about them. *What were their apartment numbers? Where did they go to school?* he wondered. But Jaime didn't know English and all he could do was stare. He was so pleased when a boy with bright red hair gave him a happy smile.

Finally, the elevator stopped at his floor once more. When the door opened, there was his mother holding Marietta in her arms. She glared down at Jaime. "Where have you been?" she demanded. "I've been worried sick about you."

Jaime explained that he'd been playing on the elevator and having the best time since he came to New York. His mom became even angrier.

"The elevator is not a toy," she scolded. "It's a means of transporting people up and down this building!"

Then Jaime asked his mother if he could at least play outside in the hallway or go up and down the stairwell.

"Absolutely not!" she shouted. "This is a public hallway. Besides, you never know who's out here. You could meet a dangerous person. In fact, you're not to talk to strangers!"

Jaime reminded his mother that back in their village no one ever worried about strangers because everyone knew each other.

"That was then and this is now," she told him. "This is our new home and we have to do things differently here."

Jaime was upset and disappointed. He wanted to argue that she didn't have to worry. He couldn't talk to strangers anyway since he only spoke Spanish. But instead, he went back inside the apartment and looked out at the world sixteen floors below.

It was cold and windy, and the sky was cloudy and gray. A fire engine screamed and cars honked their way through a traffic jam. Jaime put his hands over his ears, trying to block out the noise.

This is just like being in prison with no way to escape, he thought.

To cheer him up, Jaime's dad brought him a little present every day. He had gotten puzzles, miniature trucks and cars, and a few games. Some of the games looked interesting, but he had no one to play with. There was only Marietta, who wasn't much fun. She mostly talked to her doll, Pepita. When he tried to play with his little sister, she'd grab his toys and laugh as if it was a joke. He wished he could have someone to talk to instead of silly Marietta.

Jaime thought about the wonderful warm

climate back home. He also thought about his friends. Right now they must all be playing together and laughing and having a great time.

Tears began to fill his eyes. He looked around at his room. It was painted a light gray. His father had promised that as soon as he had time, they would paint it lemon-yellow just as his old room had been.

"But even changing the color is not going to make it feel like my *real* home," sighed Jaime. "Nothing can." Even the toys and games that lined his shelves couldn't make Jaime feel any better. In fact, right now Jaime felt lonelier than he ever had before.

3

A FAMILY OUTING

FOR THEIR FIRST two weeks in New York, Jaime and his family stayed indoors nursing the colds and sore throats they caught from the cold weather. But as soon as they were well again, they all set out to see the big city.

Jaime had never worn so many clothes in his life. He put on long underwear, two pairs of socks, an extra-heavy sweater under his coat, then a long muffler with gloves, and even a hat with earmuffs.

"I hate all these clothes," he complained. "It feels like I can't even walk."

"Never mind," said his mom. "When you get outside you'll be glad to have such nice warm clothes on."

Outside, as icy winds lashed out from behind the tall buildings and nearly knocked him over, Jaime realized his mom was right. Even with all of the clothes he was wearing, he still shivered against the biting cold. He held his father's hand tightly as they walked along a noisy, busy avenue. His mom pushed Marietta in her stroller.

"Jaime," said his dad. "You're going to see a lot of famous places that you've seen on TV, like Rockefeller Center. But first we'll take a train to get to Manhattan."

"We'll also see the beautiful Christmas window displays in the big stores along Fifth Avenue," added his mom.

Was he really going to visit places he'd seen on TV? He followed along, fascinated by all the stores and cars and people he saw. In fact, he'd never seen so many people in his whole life!

At the street corner, his mom held Marietta while his father folded her stroller. Then his father led him down a stairwell and through a tunnel under the sidewalk. He gave Jaime a special subway token to put into the coin slot and pushed him through a turnstile and onto a platform crowded with people. There were so many people that he could barely move. His arms were pinned down by the

crush of people who swept him along with the crowd. When Jaime looked around, he suddenly realized that he couldn't find his dad.

"Papi, where are you?" cried Jaime. "Mami . . . where are you?"

Jaime panicked; his parents were nowhere in sight. The platform was filled with rumbling and crashing noises. Suddenly, out of a dark tunnel, a big train with bright lights rushed into the station, and the people pushed toward the edge of the platform. Jaime's heart pounded. He still couldn't see his parents.

"Mami! Papi!" he heard himself scream. But just before he was about to burst into tears, Jaime felt his dad's strong arms lift him up to safety as the train screeched to a halt.

"It's all right, son," said his dad. "We've been right here all the time. We called out but you didn't hear us."

As they boarded the train car, Marietta began laughing and clapping. Jaime began to calm down and gave a big sigh of relief.

"You were never out of our sight for one minute! There was no need to be frightened," said his mother who was still holding Marietta. "See . . . your sister's not afraid."

Jaime shrugged; he knew that was because Marietta was too silly to care.

"These underground trains beneath the city take people to different places," explained his dad as though nothing scary had happened. "Remember, I told you that they're called 'subways' in English. What a marvelous place this is. We're lucky to live here!"

So far, it definitely didn't feel like a marvelous place to Jaime.

When they arrived at their subway stop, Jaime held on tightly to his dad's hand. After the incident on the subway platform he wasn't taking any chances. They walked up many stairwells and out into the street.

The tall buildings seemed to reach up into the sky and mingle with the clouds. He had thought that only mountains could reach up that high.

When they got to Rockefeller Center, Jaime pointed to the huge Christmas tree filled with bright lights and shouted, "That must be the biggest tree in the whole world!"

"And here's the ice-skating rink we saw on television," announced his dad.

The large rink was packed with skaters, just as it had appeared on television. Only now, this close up, Jaime saw that many of them were kids. Some wore colorful outfits. They raced and glided along on ice skates while happy music filled the rink.

"They look like they are floating on air!" cried Jaime as he looked down from the promenade.

The skaters turned, swirled and some even did acrobatic movements. It all looked so magical and beautiful.

"Boy! I wish I could skate like them!" Jaime told his parents.

"Not today," said his father. But his parents promised that once they were more settled, they would buy him a pair of ice skates.

"Can I have them for Christmas?" he asked.

"Not this Christmas, Jaime; we still have things to buy for our apartment," said his dad.

"Jaime," said his mom, "we're going to have a very simple celebration this Christmas. So don't expect much. You must learn to be patient. We just moved here. Things take time."

That was not the answer he wanted to hear.

Later, they went window-shopping along Fifth Avenue. All the large stores had their windows decorated with colorful Christmas displays of winter scenes. Jaime was amazed and delighted when he saw Santa Claus and the elves, gingerbread houses and all kinds of mannequins, puppets and toys on exhibit.

"Look!" he shouted and stepped up against the large window. Back home Jaime and his classmates had read a picture book about winter. The story was about a boy and his shiny red sled. "It's the sled . . . the one in my book!" exclaimed Jaime. "Please can I have it? Please? I want to play in the snow with my sled — just like in our book!"

"But there's no snow," said his mom. The winter had been cold but no snow had fallen yet.

"Let's wait until we get some snow first,"

said his dad. "Then we'll see about a sled. Remember that you still have to be registered in school and there's much we have to do. But I'm glad to see there are some things you like about our new home. Someday you'll realize what a lucky boy you are."

"Maybe you'll stop complaining so much about living in New York City," said his mom.

"He'll be fine, just fine," his dad told his mom. "Won't you, son?"

Jaime nodded, but he wasn't so sure.

Later that night as he lay in bed, Jaime thought about the kids in the skating rink who looked so happy as they raced and spun around. But even the skates he liked and the neat red sled would probably never be his. Now that he was back in the apartment he wondered when he would get to go outside again. He felt as if everything he wanted or liked was out of his reach. Jaime began to feel sad and lonely all over again.

4

THE MAGIC SHELL

ANOTHER WEEK passed in New York City, and things were as boring as ever for Jaime. His dad was busy working every day and didn't have time to take Jaime out with him. His mom was busy fixing up their large apartment and taking care of little Marietta who had caught another cold.

Jaime found himself stuck indoors and without friends. He was becoming more and more restless and unhappy. One morning at breakfast, he complained to his dad.

"I have no one to play with. I don't understand this language. I want to go back home!"

"This is your home now and you'd better get used to living here," commanded his dad.

"So that's that! We don't want to hear you whine anymore."

"In a few weeks your records should be here from the Dominican Republic. Then you're going to school," his mother reminded Jaime. "You'll learn English and meet other children and make friends."

"And in the meantime, I'll teach you to say a few words," said his father, who was the only one in the family who could speak English.

Jaime nodded sadly; after all, what else could he do?

"Jaime, look on the bright side," said his mom. "Even though we're not having a big Christmas this year, you'll be having a birthday at the beginning of March. We'll have a party for you. You might get those skates or that sled you wanted. I know you'll like that."

Jaime knew she was trying to cheer him up but it didn't work. It only reminded him of how lonely he was.

"How can I go skating or sledding and have a party without any friends?" protested

Jaime. They had been in New York City for almost three weeks and he had not made a single friend. "I hate it here! I hate it! I do, I do!" he shouted, then ran to his room and slammed his door.

His parents looked at each other helplessly. It seemed there was no way to make their son happy.

"Why am I in this terrible place, trapped indoors?" sighed Jaime as he sat miserably on his bed.

He thought about his wonderful village where he was free to run and play. He wondered what Wilfredo, Lucy and Sarita were doing right now, at this very moment.

Just then he spotted the box that Tío Ernesto had given him. It sat on top of his desk. *How did it get there?* he wondered. Jaime had put the box away when they first arrived and never gave it another thought. He hadn't even seen it since they'd moved in. Now here it was!

Jaime opened the box and took out the conch shell. He turned it over and examined it carefully. It didn't look very special to

Jaime. In fact, it looked quite ordinary.

But as Jaime held the shell, Tío Ernesto's words came back to him . . . as if his great-uncle was right in his room speaking:

> . . . *All of your memories are stored inside this shell. When you become homesick for Montaña Verde this special shell will comfort you. You must be quiet and concentrate and listen carefully. You will hear the roaring sea and soon you will have memories of home — of our mountain village, where the skies touch heaven and the earth smiles down at the sea.*

Jaime held the shell up to his ear, just as Tío Ernesto had shown him. At first he heard nothing. But soon he began to hear the splashing waves — then the roaring sea. The shell fluttered gently in his hands. Then it began to sparkle. Soon its glow got brighter and brighter until a rainbow appeared. Streaks of golden light swept across the ceiling and floor.

He felt the carpet vibrate, and blades of grass sprouted up from under his slippers.

Trees appeared, and Jaime felt the warm sunshine and smelled the sweetness of honeysuckle and jasmine. Birds chirped and bees gathered pollen from the flowers. . . .

"Hey, Jaime, let's play tag!" Wilfredo tapped Jaime's shoulder and shouted, "Tocao, you're it!" Lucy and Sarita called out to him. Jaime raced to the top of the hill and tagged Sarita who tagged Wilfredo. They ran and laughed and chased each other along the path up to Tío Ernesto's cabin. Tío Ernesto invited them inside for some cool, sweet lemonade, made with lemons from his lemon tree.

Jaime swung in the hammock while his friends sat on wooden stools. Tío Ernesto had often told them stories about his worldly travels. His cabin was filled with lots of artifacts from his journeys around the world. Today, he held up a large ceremonial mask. "This is from the west coast of Africa. Many of our ancestors were brought here from West Africa by the Spaniards as captive slaves." Then Jaime picked up his favorite wooden carving. Every

time he visited his great-uncle's cabin, he al-
ways played with the statue of the little boy
sitting on a rock fishing in the river.

"I made that carving myself, right here," Tío
Ernesto told them.

Jaime really loved that carving. It always
made him feel good just to hold it.

"Jaime . . . Jaime! What are you doing,
son?" He heard his mother's voice.

When Jaime blinked, there was his mother
standing beside him. Once again everything
in his room was just as before.

"What are you doing playing with that
conch shell?" she asked.

Jaime saw that his shell had become ordinary again.

"Tío Ernesto gave it to me as a going-away present."

"What a strange gift! What are you going to do with it?" she asked.

"I'm going to keep it for good luck," he said and put his shell safely away.

Every day after that, Jaime went into his room and closed the door. He would listen to the roaring sea and wait for the shell to take him back to Montaña Verde. There he played *la gallinita ciega*, blindman's buff. He played *escondido*, hide-and-go-seek. He followed his friends to the shallow riverbed to catch tadpoles. He ate delicious homemade *dulce de leche*, milk candy. Jaime was home once more, and he was very happy.

Soon his parents began to worry. "You spend too much time in your room," they kept telling him. But Jaime wouldn't listen to them. He was busy having great adventures with his best buddies in the warm sunshine of Montaña Verde.

5

MAKING NEW FRIENDS

WHEN JAIME woke up on Christmas morning, he was excited. He ran into the living room expecting to find lots of presents just as he had every Christmas back home. But all he saw were two stockings, one for him and one for Marietta. More than anything, Jaime had wished for his sled or the ice skates, or some other great surprise. But instead, he got a new truck, some clothes and a new schoolbag with pencils, a sharpener and an eraser. It was hard to hide his disappointment.

"It's for when you go to your new school," his mother said.

"Stop sulking," his father scolded. "You don't know how lucky you are. Living in this fine apartment and having toys to spare. There are kids who go hungry and have nothing and never even own a toy. So, cut it out!"

Jaime was tired of his father always telling him how lucky he was. He didn't have one friend, and he didn't feel lucky at all. If it weren't for his shell, Jaime would really have been miserable.

One morning just as he finished another wonderful visit to Montaña Verde and was putting away his shell, he heard loud voices from the kitchen.

"All he does is stay in his room. We must do something with that boy!" shouted his father. "Jaime's got to get out of this apartment and into the fresh air."

His mother agreed and they decided that from now on she would take him out for a walk every day. Jaime wasn't happy about that and still griped about all the clothes he had to wear. "I can't move and I don't want to play by myself."

"Never mind," insisted his mom, "the cold makes your cheeks rosy. Besides, I must go shopping and take Marietta for her walk and you cannot stay alone."

Jaime shrugged; he knew he had to go whether he liked it or not.

On their way back from shopping that afternoon, Jaime spotted some kids running and having fun in the playground inside their apartment complex.

"Let's go into the playground," said his mom, hoping to get Jaime interested in playing outdoors. "I'd like to put Marietta on the swings."

"Okay," said Jaime. His mom was pleased he agreed and found an empty bench on the sunny side of the playground.

Jaime spotted the kid with red hair who had smiled at him in the elevator. The kid stopped bouncing his ball when he seemed to notice Jaime, too. He slowly edged his way over, and the two boys smiled at each other.

The boy continued bouncing his ball as if he were waiting for Jaime to say something. But Jaime suddenly became shy. *What could I say to him?* he thought. *After all, I can't speak English.*

Jaime watched, disappointed, as the boy ran off to play with the other boys.

"I think that boy wants to play with you," said his mother.

"But, what can I do about it?" he asked.

"You could say 'hello.' Your father has taught you a few words of English. Why don't you try it out?" urged his mom.

But Jaime had not been very cooperative whenever his dad attempted to teach him English. Now he was sorry he hadn't paid attention.

Just then the ball rolled over to the bench where he was sitting with his mom. Jaime grabbed it and threw it back.

"Thanks!" yelled the boy and waved at Jaime who waved back.

"There," said his mom, "why don't you go over and play?"

"No, I don't want to," answered Jaime. "What if they don't like me?"

"I know that boy likes you," she said.

But Jaime was feeling too shy about going over to the kids he didn't know and insisted on going home.

At dinner that evening he spoke to his dad. "Dad, help me again with my English."

"That's my boy!" said his dad who was very pleased that Jaime was finally taking an interest in learning English. After they finished dinner, his dad taught him to say, "Hello, my name is Jaime," and "How are you? I'm fine," and "Good-bye."

The next afternoon, his mother took Jaime back to the playground, but when he saw that none of the kids were there, he was disappointed. He pushed Marietta on the swings and waited. After a while he took her back to the bench where his mom sat.

"Might as well go home," he told his mom. Just as they were about to leave, he saw the friendly redheaded boy arrive with the other children. This time he waved to Jaime, and a few minutes later he came over.

Bouncing his ball a few times, the boy smiled at Jaime. "Hi! I'm Peter. Who are you?"

Jaime understood. He pointed to himself and tried to answer just as his dad had taught him.

"Hello. *Me llamo Jaime.* Jaime!"

Peter turned to his friends and explained

that Jaime didn't speak English. They all nodded their heads and smiled at Jaime.

"You want to play, Jaime?" asked Peter and pointed to Jaime, then himself, and then signaled toward the other kids.

"Go on, Jaime," coaxed his mom. "Go on. He wants you to play."

"Come on," said Peter and motioned with his hand for Jaime to come along with him.

"Go on and play," his mom urged Jaime. "We'll be right here if you want to come back. Marietta is happy in her stroller."

Jaime rushed off with Peter. They went to the monkey bars. Peter pointed to each kid and called out their names.

"This is Kevin and Gina and Sheila. His name is Jaime."

Jaime was so excited that he couldn't remember any of their names.

"Let's play follow the leader," said Kevin. "Follow me!" yelled Peter.

Jaime didn't understand what they said, but he followed the others and copied whatever they did. He climbed the monkey bars, went on the seesaw, took giant steps. It was so much fun.

"What school do you go to?" Kevin asked Jaime.

Jaime shrugged. He understood that Kevin was asking something about his school. But he did not know how to answer.

"Jaime can't speak English too good," said Peter. "I heard his mom talking to him in Spanish. I think he only speaks Spanish."

Jaime smiled. "Spanish, *sí, sí,*" he said, nodding. Then the kids said something else and everyone laughed. Jaime laughed, too, although he didn't know what was said. All he knew was that he hadn't had this much fun since he'd moved to New York.

All too soon, Jaime heard his mother calling. It was already time to go home. He wanted to play some more and asked his mother if they could stay a little longer. But she told him it was time to go home so she could start making supper.

"Come out and play again, Jaime," said Peter. "See you!" yelled the kids.

"See you," echoed Jaime. Then he remembered his lessons with his dad and added, "Good-bye. I'm fine!" The children laughed and laughed.

Jaime smiled and waved. They made him so happy.

That night, when Jaime went to bed, he could hardly wait to see his friends again the next day.

On the very next afternoon as his mom was getting Marietta ready to go out to the playground, Jaime looked out of his window. Something was different. Snowflakes filled the air! They fell, swirling and dancing before his eyes! The city was being covered in a blanket of snow.

It never snowed in Montaña Verde. It was a tropical climate and too hot for snow. Even on Christmas you could play in the warm sunshine and go swimming.

Jaime had seen snow in books and pictures, but he'd never seen the real thing. Back home, everyone had only talked about snow. There was a popular folktale, told to the kids by the storytellers of the Spanish Caribbean. It was about how snow came to be. Many kids believed it to be true. "Snow is magic," the story went, "because when the Sun God is asleep, the angels in heaven get very cold and they cry. Their tears freeze into flakes. As the flakes fall to earth they turn into snow.

"When the Sun God wakes up the snow melts. The angels become warm again and smile. Until next time."

Some of the kids believed snow was really magic and so had Jaime. But his dad had told him that snow was not magic. He explained that snow was formed from the vapor of frozen water high up in the atmosphere.

Jaime had listened but he had not understood all of what his dad had told him. He still wondered if the story about the angels really could be true. Sometimes Jaime would stare at the clouds, searching to see if he could find any angels.

"Is snow really magic?" he whispered. Now he would see for himself!

Jaime rushed to find his mother and little sister and hurry them along.

"Snow! Mami . . . snow!" Marietta laughed and pointed outside. The city was covered in white.

His mom dressed Marietta and made sure Jaime had on his muffler and boots. Then they all went outdoors and headed over to the playground.

Jaime felt his heart beating. How would the snowflakes feel? How would they taste?

He removed a glove and felt the gentle flakes melt instantly in his hand.

They looked like the drops of morning mist that fell over Montaña Verde during sunrise. Jaime licked his palm and tasted cold fresh water just like in the riverbed back home.

When he got to the playground, Jaime heard the kids calling out his name. They waved and he waved back as he slid and slipped over to them.

All afternoon they chased each other and tumbled onto a cushion of powdery snow. They tried to make snow people, but the snow was too soft. Jaime, Peter and Kevin even had a soft snowball fight against Sheila and Gina.

"Isn't this fun?" yelled Peter.

"Isn't this fun?" mimicked Jaime.

"You're a funny kid!" said Sheila, and Jaime laughed along with all the other kids.

This was just as great as playing back home with his buddies. What was even better was that all of the kids lived in the same apartment complex. That meant they could meet in the playground and play together every day.

Later that night, just before he fell asleep, Jaime thought about his shell. But when he went to find the box it was nowhere to be seen. Jaime yawned; he was too tired to search for the shell.

"I'm also too tired to visit Montaña Verde right now," yawned Jaime, and he dozed off into a deep sleep.

That night he dreamed about riding a shiny red sled in the snow and racing along on a pair of super ice skates with all of his new friends.

6

NEW FRIENDS,
NEW SCHOOL

FOR THE NEXT two months Jaime met his friends almost every afternoon at the playground. They played and hung out together. And each day he learned more new words and new phrases in English and made fewer mistakes.

Soon he was talking freely with the other children. Jaime even taught them some Spanish words.

"*Mira* means look," he told them. "*Bueno* means good."

Now when the kids played tag, they'd shout, "*¡Mira, mira!*" Or, when one of them won at hopscotch, they'd call out, "*¡Bueno, bueno!*"

Jaime enjoyed playing with Kevin, Gina and Sheila. But it was Peter who became his best friend.

Peter lived in Jaime's building on the eighth floor. The boys were allowed to visit each other frequently. It was great to just hop on the elevator and visit with Peter. And it was wonderful to have a best friend again.

Jaime liked to play with Peter's Nintendo games. Peter enjoyed building things with Jaime's huge Lego set.

Their mothers became friends, too. Mrs. Shaw, Peter's mom, helped Jaime's mom with her English homework. In return she tutored Mrs. Shaw in Spanish. Jaime's mom had worked as a nurse in the Dominican Republic. Now she was studying English two nights a week at the local high school.

"As soon as I become fluent in English I'll apply for my license to practice nursing," she told Mrs. Shaw. "By then my family should be quite settled here."

"I studied Spanish in school but forgot most of it," Mrs. Shaw told Jaime's mom. "Now it's all coming back. And we can talk together in two languages. How wonderful!"

Jaime's mom taught Mrs. Shaw how to make *dulce de coco*, coconut candy. And Mrs.

Shaw taught his mom how to bake brownies.

The two women spent time together and on occasion the families shared coffee and dessert. They were all becoming good friends.

"That Mrs. Shaw is a nice woman," his mother told him. "No wonder Peter is such an agreeable boy."

By early February, Jaime's records finally arrived from the Dominican Republic.

"Here they are at last!" said his dad, holding the big manila envelope. "Monday you will start school."

Jaime was put in the second grade instead of the third grade with all of his friends. He was disappointed because the kids in his class were younger. "Well, at least they won't tease you," Peter told him. "Since you're older they know you can beat them up."

This was true and it did make Jaime feel better.

"This is only temporary," Mr. Phillips, the principal, told his parents. "Your son is a bright boy. As soon as his English is up to standard he'll be placed in his proper grade."

In the meantime, Jaime was also getting special tutoring in English every afternoon.

In his tutoring session there were two other children. One was a girl named Kim who was from South Korea and the other was a boy named Alberto who was from Colombia in South America.

Jaime liked school. He especially enjoyed working with Mr. Salas, his tutor. Mr. Salas told them that they must each present an oral report about their home country. Their work had to include a map and pictures.

Kim told them about Seoul, the capital of South Korea. "Seoul is a very big city and crowded with lots of people and buildings," she said, pointing to a large map of South Korea. She also showed pictures from magazines. "It's like New York City. The winters are very cold, just like here."

"Bogotá, where I was born, is the capital

of Colombia," said Alberto. He brought in a map of all of South America. "Bogotá is a large city, but not so big like New York. The weather is never cold, and it never gets too hot. My dad says that it's always like the springtime here in New York City." Alberto had lots of photographs to show.

Jaime talked about his village in the Dominican Republic. He, too, brought magazine pictures and photographs from back home. He held out a map of the Dominican Republic.

"I lived in a village up in the highlands in the north. The biggest city in the north is Puerto Plata. It is not too far. Santo Domingo, the capital, is the largest city in our country," he said. "I used to visit my cousins who live there. Our weather back home is warm. Sometimes it gets very hot, although it's always cool in the mountains. But you never need a coat or a muffler and gloves . . . like here."

After their tutoring sessions, the kids had some free time. That's when Jaime and

Alberto got together to talk. Jaime enjoyed talking to Alberto. It had been a long time since Jaime had someone his own age that he could talk to in Spanish. Alberto's neighborhood was a few miles away from where Jaime lived. He lived in a section of Queens where there were many Latinos. It had *bodegas,*

small grocery stores, and lots of Caribbean restaurants.

"You would like it, Jaime. Mostly everyone speaks Spanish," said Alberto.

Jaime did know the area because his parents shopped there on weekends.

"My mom was happy when she found out about that neighborhood," Jaime told Alberto. "She loves to buy her plantains, mangos and all the other groceries she needs to make Dominican food, just like back home. My dad even rents movie videos in Spanish from the stores in your neighborhood."

"So then why didn't your parents move to our neighborhood?" Alberto asked Jaime.

"My father said that he had to live near his job. It was his company that got us our apartment and our car," explained Jaime. "Besides, I like where we live. There's a neat playground. And I made good friends. Hey, maybe you can come to my house, Alberto. I'll ask my mother."

When Jaime spoke to his mother, she reminded him that he was having a birthday soon.

"Why don't you invite Alberto to your party?"

"May I invite Kim, too?" he asked.

"You may invite all of your friends," answered his mom.

"All right!" cried Jaime. Now, as far as he was concerned, this was great news.

7

¡*FELIZ CUMPLEAÑOS!*
HAPPY BIRTHDAY

BY THE TIME Jaime's birthday came around he had a great bunch of kids to play with and a new best friend. English was becoming easier and easier for him. There were now moments when he even thought in English.

Once in a while, though, Jaime remembered Wilfredo, Lucy and Sarita and even imagined how much his old friends would enjoy playing in the snow. Whenever he planned to write to them he was always busy with his friends or working hard at school so he could be promoted to the third grade.

Some nights when Jaime was alone in his room, he did think about Tío Ernesto and did plan to take out his shell and visit home again.

But somehow he always forgot. In fact, lately, he hardly ever thought about Montaña Verde.

In time, Tío Ernesto and the shell were altogether forgotten.

When Jaime heard the doorbell he was ready and waiting and quickly opened the door.

"Happy birthday!" shouted Peter, who was the first one to arrive. Today was Saturday — Jaime's birthday celebration.

Soon the doorbell rang again and it was Sheila and Gina. Then later Kevin, Alberto and Kim arrived all at once.

"Everybody's here," announced Jaime. "It's time for my party to begin!"

They all ate pizza, which was Jaime's favorite American food, hot dogs and cheeseburgers.

They blew up balloons and played *escondido* and *la gallinita ciega*. Alberto won at musical chairs, since he was the last one seated.

Finally, Jaime's mom brought out a big chocolate birthday cake. Everyone sang "Happy Birthday." Then Jaime's parents along with Alberto sang *"Feliz cumpleaños,"* as the others tried to sing along in Spanish.

"Make a wish!" everyone shouted.

Jaime closed his eyes and wished for the red sled he had seen in the store window and a pair of shiny ice skates. Then he took a deep breath and blew out all the candles.

Jaime and his friends stuffed themselves with birthday cake, ice cream and *dulce de maní,* delicious sweet peanut candy. It was Jaime's favorite. His mother had made it herself. Everyone was having a wonderful time.

When it was time to open his presents, his mom handed him a small parcel. "Open this first," she said. "It's from Tío Ernesto."

Jaime read the card from his great-uncle.

"Montaña Verde remembers you. Feliz cumpleaños, *Tío Ernesto."*

When he unwrapped the parcel, he could hardly believe his eyes. Tío Ernesto had sent him his favorite wooden carving of the boy fishing in the river. Jaime held it in his hands and felt very happy. It was like having Tío Ernesto right there with him on his birthday.

He opened his other presents and got books, puzzles, a fire engine truck and clothes. But the best presents were from his parents: a shiny new red sled and a pair of ice skates with bright silver blades!

Jaime could hardly believe it. Not only had he gotten the red sled but he got the ice skates, too! "Great!" he shouted. The sled was just like the one in the store window, and the skates looked exactly like the ones he had seen on the skaters.

"Maybe next week we'll take you to Rockefeller Center," said his mom, "and you can try out your new skates."

"Tomorrow, I'll take you to the park and you can try out your sled," his father told him.

"Can I bring Peter?" Jaime asked.

"Sure," replied his dad, pleased to see his son so cheerful.

Jaime did feel very joyful indeed. It was the best birthday party he had ever had.

In bed that night Jaime admired his new toys. He reached out to touch his shiny new sled and knocked over the wooden carving that Tío Ernesto had sent. Luckily it didn't break.

As Jaime picked up the carving, he felt as if he was going to search for tadpoles in the riverbed with all of his friends. He even saw Montaña Verde, Tío Ernesto's wooden cabin and all his friends drinking sweet lemonade. *If only Wilfredo, Lucy and Sarita could see me now,* thought Jaime. *What would they think?*

Suddenly he had an urge to go back, to visit Montaña Verde and to be with his friends once more.

Quickly he began to look for his shell. It had been a very long time since he had used it and he didn't even remember where it was. After searching all over his room, he found the box in the back of his closet.

Jaime sat listening to the shell. But all was quiet. There was no roaring of the sea, no glow or rainbow. Nothing changed.

He tried again and again. But everything remained the same. He just sat holding his shell and waiting. Finally, he felt too exhausted to go on.

As he sat on his bed with his shell next to him, he whispered, "Maybe I'll try again tomorrow. Maybe I'll even write to my friends like I promised."

Jaime lay his head down on his pillow and began thinking about all of the things he would write to them. And soon he fell fast asleep.

8

A BIG SURPRISE

THE NEXT MORNING when Jaime woke up he was surprised to find the shell in front of the closet door. But he was too excited and busy getting ready to go to the park with his dad and Peter to think much of it, so he put the shell away in his closet once more.

"I don't have time now. I'll try again another day," he said and left to go sledding.

Jaime had a wonderful time in the snow. He and Peter took turns riding his red sled. Jaime's dad helped push them over the snow-covered park slopes.

Later that afternoon, while Jaime was putting away all of his new presents, he once more picked up the carving of the little boy fishing at the river. Again he thought of all the fun he'd had searching for tadpoles and wading in the river.

"I want to write to my friends back home," he told himself. He asked his parents right then if he could buy some picture postcards.

"Wonderful, Jaime. I'm glad to hear that you remember the folks back home," said his mom. "Aunt Carmen and Uncle Manuel tell us in their letters that your friends always ask about you."

That afternoon Jaime went shopping with his family. He got three picture postcards, one for each of his friends. Each card showed a famous site in New York City.

He sent the one of the Empire State Building to Wilfredo. "Here's where King Kong was supposed to have climbed up," he wrote. "Just like in the movie."

The Twin Towers card was for Lucy. "It's as high as our mountains. I can see far out for miles and miles over two other states."

On the Rockefeller Center card, he wrote Sarita, "Here's where I'm going to go skating with my new ice skates."

Jaime told them about his plane ride and about his new friends. But the most exciting news was that he had played in the snow. He knew they would really like to hear about that.

He examined what he wrote on his post-cards and was satisfied that he could reach out to his friends without the shell. They would know he still remembered them. Jaime happily mailed his postcards.

During the next few weeks there was lots to do. There were several snowfalls. Jaime played with his friends and shared his red sled.

His dad took him and Peter to the big rink in Rockefeller Center. Jaime put on his skates and after falling a few times learned how to stay up.

In time he was skating around, racing and spinning, just like Peter and the other children.

By early springtime, Jaime was promoted to the third grade. He was very happy when he saw that Kevin and Gina were in his class.

"Your teacher tells me you're doing well," said his mother.

"We're so pleased with your good grades," said his dad. "Keep them up and we'll have a special surprise for you."

Jaime asked what this surprise would be. But his parents looked at each other, smiled and said nothing.

Jaime couldn't stop wondering what the surprise was. But he was too busy to stay curious. He had to meet Peter and his friends at the playground.

One day his mother handed him some envelopes. "Here, Jaime, these letters are for you."

Jaime saw that they were from his friends. It was exciting to receive news from back home, and his heart beat fast as he read their letters.

Everyone wrote that they missed him very much. Especially Wilfredo.

"On Independence Day, February 27th, we went down to Puerto Plata. We saw the carnival parades. People wore super masks and costumes. The musicians played lots of great music," wrote Wilfredo. "I hung out with the kids. But it was not the same without you." He even included snapshots of the dancers and other carnival events.

"Was snow really tasteless?" asked Lucy in her letter. Lucy had sent him more snapshots of herself and the other kids.

"Please send us some pictures of you in the snow," wrote Sarita. She had sent him some of her crayon drawings. Sarita loved to draw.

Jaime was pleased to know that they still remembered and missed him.

His parents gave him some snapshots to send to his friends. They showed Jaime playing in the snow with his new friends. There was one of his new sled. Another photograph showed him ice-skating with Peter on the big rink at Rockefeller Center.

"I wish I could see them again. Do you think we can ever go back to visit?" he asked.

His parents looked at each other and laughed as if they were sharing a big secret.

"Jaime," said his mom, "you might as well

know now as well as later. When school is over we are all going back home for a long visit!"

Jaime could hardly believe what he had heard. "Home? To Montaña Verde?" he asked.

"Yes," said his dad. "My company is sending me to work on a project in Puerto Plata. That means we'll be there for most of the summer! So you can write and tell your friends that you will be seeing them in person soon."

Jaime wrote his letters and included his photographs. In each letter, he signed off by saying, "I'll see you in person in less than a month!"

"Tomorrow I'll show these pictures from back home to Peter and the kids," he said.

Jaime could not have been happier.

9

SAYING GOOD-BYE
AGAIN

IT WAS THE very last day of school. In a few days, Jaime and his family would be flying back to Montaña Verde, for a visit.

Most of his friends, including Peter, were going to the Discovery Summer Day Camp.

"Too bad you can't come," said Peter.

"There's a great big swimming pool. Last year, Peter and me had a swimming race against two other boys," said Kevin. "They almost beat us, too, until one of the boys, Johnnie, got a cramp. The counselor said it was from stuffing his fat mouth with too much watermelon before he went into the water. Anyway, it slowed them up."

"Yeah," agreed Peter, "and we won the race!" He gave Kevin a high five.

"We make our own wood fires there," said Sheila.

"And cook hot dogs and hamburgers," said Gina.

"My favorite are the roasted marshmallows on a stick. The marshmallows get nice and burnt on the outside and soft and gooey on the inside. Yum, yummy," Sheila said and smacked her lips.

"That's right," agreed Peter. "Everything we cook tastes better there."

As they talked about all their good times in camp last summer, Jaime felt left out.

"I'll be doing some neat stuff back home, too," he told them. But the kids didn't seem interested. They were too busy remembering all of last year's camp activities.

Jaime listened and thought about all the fun he would be missing.

"I wish I could go to Discovery Summer Day Camp with you guys, too," he told them.

"Too bad," said Peter. Kevin, Sheila and Gina all agreed. "Maybe next year," they said.

Jaime nodded. He was no longer so happy about going back to Montaña Verde. He already knew what he was going to do over there. While here, it was all new and exciting to him.

The more Jaime thought about Discovery Summer Day Camp, the more he sulked. One day he even lost his temper.

"Don't touch my toys," he screamed, shoving Marietta and making her cry.

"Now you must stop this," warned his mother. "Why are you so grouchy, anyway?"

But Jaime never answered; he just stomped off to his room.

"Why do I have to go?" he asked himself. "I'm happy here now. I've made such good friends. I don't want to go back to Montaña Verde," he grumbled and kicked a truck across his bedroom.

Each day he became more touchy.

Finally, his dad had a serious talk with him.

"Jaime, you must stop behaving like a brat. What's wrong? We're going to be leaving for Montaña Verde in a few days. I should think you'd be very happy to see your friends again . . ."

"I don't want to go!" shouted Jaime. "I already have friends right here. Why can't we stay? Most of the kids are going to this great summer day camp. That's where I want to go."

"That's impossible," said his dad. "We have made our plans and we're leaving."

"But I'll miss out on some great fun, Dad . . ."

"We're coming back," answered his dad. "It's not like we're staying in Montaña Verde for good. Perhaps next summer you can go to summer camp."

But Jaime folded his arms and sat sulking.

"Now stop acting silly," said his mother. "First you didn't want to stay here. Now you don't want to return just for a visit."

"I think you're being greedy," said his father. "You want to have your friends and family miss you in Montaña Verde, and you want to stay and play in camp with your new friends."

His dad looked angry and he shook his finger at Jaime.

"Selfish people who want it all sometimes get nothing. Family and friends are looking forward to our visit. How about thinking about their feelings, young man?"

His parents were so annoyed with Jaime that they sent him to his room for the rest of the evening.

Jaime sat on his bed and tried to think about the fun he used to have with Wilfredo and his friends back in his village.

But things had changed. He was used to his friends, his neighborhood and his school in Queens, New York. What if his friends here got used to him being away? What if they didn't want to be friends when he got back?

Jaime couldn't help wishing he could stay and go to camp with Peter, Kevin, Sheila and Gina.

Finally the day came and Jaime had to help pack his things. When he opened his closet door, he tripped over the box with the conch shell. Jaime shoved the box into the back of his closet.

A little later when he sat on his bed he felt a hard lump. Jaime pushed back his quilt and there was the box . . . again! "I thought I put this away," he murmured, scratching his head.

Jaime opened the box. The shell was inside, looking plain and ordinary. He thought a while, then decided to pick it up and try once more to hear the sea. He concentrated and waited.

Nothing happened.

"Useless old thing!" Jaime said and became annoyed with the shell.

But when he went to put it back into the box it was almost as though it jumped out of his hands.

"Something's odd here," he whispered. "I'll take this back to Montaña Verde with me. That way I can ask Tío Ernesto all about this curious shell."

The shell did not move an inch when Jaime finally packed it away in his suitcase.

10

MONTAÑA VERDE

AUNT CARMEN and Uncle Manuel were waiting at the airport. Jaime had to wait for all of the hugging and kissing and crying to finish.

He gave a sigh of relief when they all got into his uncle's green Jeep and headed up the winding road to his village.

"Jaime, eat some of my homemade *dulce de maní*," said Aunt Carmen, handing him a generous piece. "I made it especially for you."

"My favorite!" shouted Jaime and bit off a big chunk. The sweet peanut flavor filled his mouth as he ate the crunchy candy.

"I hear you're speaking English like a real Yankee, Jaime," his Uncle Manuel laughed.

"Even Marietta says lots of words in English now," said his mother.

"I hope she never forgets our language," said Aunt Carmen.

"Don't worry, Carmen, we're not going to let Jaime or Marietta forget the Dominican Republic, where they were born. They're going to continue to speak like Dominicans," his dad assured her.

"Pedro and I will always speak to our kids in Spanish," added his mom. "We're also going to make sure that they continue to read and write in our language."

"Besides," said his dad, "we'll be sending them back to Montaña Verde during vacation time in the years to come. Nothing will be lost."

Jaime hardly listened as the grown-ups chattered on and shared the latest news. It was all so quiet. So different from life in New York City. No traffic here, or streets filled with people.

He inhaled deeply, enjoying the familiar tangy and sweet smells of the tropical countryside. Colorful wildflowers grew along the hilltops and then scattered down to the edge of the road. Birds chirped and flew down along the treetops by the narrow paths. Clusters of butterflies bounced over the wild-flowers. The skies were a brilliant blue and the bright hot sun made everything sparkle.

Jaime felt the cool mountain breeze coming in through the car window. He had forgotten how beautiful it was in the Dominican Republic. He had forgotten how much he loved these beautiful mountains of the north.

Finally, they drove off the main highway and onto the long twisting road that climbed up to Montaña Verde.

When they arrived at his uncle's, Jaime saw his bike waiting for him by the side of the house.

"Great!" he shouted as he jumped out of the car, hopped onto his bike, and began to ride up and down the front road. After so long, it felt wonderful to ride again.

"Jaime, take off your good clothes and freshen up first," scolded his mom. "Then you can play."

After lunch, Jaime heard the doorbell. He rushed out to find Wilfredo, Lucy and Sarita waiting for him.

"Jaime! Look, it's Jaime!" they shouted.

"I got you guys some presents," he told them. "Let's go inside."

Jaime gave Wilfredo a fishing rod with a blue case. "We knew you could use this when you go fishing."

He gave Lucy a neat badminton set. She loved to play badminton. That was because she won most of the games.

He gave Sarita a set of watercolor paints and a pad of watercolor paper. "You can paint some great pictures," he told her.

All of them were overjoyed with their gifts.

"Now it's time to go out and play!" yelled Jaime. "It's been too long since we went to the riverbed."

"Yeah, let's catch some tadpoles," said Wilfredo.

"Hey, Jaime, let's play tag!" Lucy tapped his shoulder.

"I'll beat you all!" Sarita called out and she rushed out first.

Jaime ran up the hill after his friends.

"*Tocao!*" he screamed after tagging Sarita.

"No . . ." she giggled and then tagged Lucy. "You're it!"

"Now, this is what I call fun!" laughed Jaime.

It was wonderful to run free like this again. He looked out at the green mountains, the flowers and butterflies. He felt the soft earth underneath his sneakers. Tears of joy filled his eyes. Jaime had come back home to his mountain village. He was with his friends once more.

As the days passed, Jaime played *la gallinita ciega* and *escondido* with his friends. He traveled with his family down to the beach in Sosua where they went swimming and boating.

His older cousin Carlos tried to show him how to windsurf. At first, Jaime kept falling off the surfboard and losing the sail. But in time he got the hang of it.

"You're not that great yet," said Carlos, "but next visit when you're older you'll do better."

Jaime ate lots of sweet mangos and *dulce de maní*. He traveled with his family south to the capital to visit his Uncle Jorge and other relatives. Uncle Jorge was delighted at how quickly Jaime had learned English.

"Jaime, how do you say, 'No thank you,' or 'It's too much money,'" his Uncle Jorge teased. When Jaime answered in perfect English, everyone laughed. "That's some smart kid." His relatives agreed.

This pleased Jaime and he told Uncle Jorge and the others all about New York City. He spoke about his school and told about playing in the snow with his friends. All of this talk made Jaime remember New York.

Back in Puerto Plata, he had already sent Peter and the others some neat picture post-cards. Now he wondered what Peter, Sheila, Kevin, Gina and the other kids were doing. Were they having fun at the day camp? He knew he would not see them again until summer was almost over.

But as Jaime went on with his wonderful vacation he forgot all about New York.

When he returned to Montaña Verde for the remainder of his holidays, Jaime played once more with his friends.

Then one morning Jaime heard the roosters crowing. He woke up as usual, but this time he went over to the wall and glanced at the calendar. He noticed the red circle around the 25th of August. He could hardly believe it. His wonderful vacation was already coming to an end. In two more days, he would be leaving for New York City.

That afternoon he invited Wilfredo, Lucy and Sarita to come and visit him in New York City for Christmas. Jaime couldn't believe it when Wilfredo's family said that a visit might be possible.

"Maybe we'll even have a white Christmas and you'll be able to see snow," Jaime said.

"Will you teach me to ice-skate?" asked Wilfredo.

"It's a deal!" agreed Jaime. Lucy and Sarita hoped that perhaps the following Christmas they could visit Jaime, too.

Now that it was time to go back to New York, Jaime kept thinking about the large buildings and the noisy traffic. New York City seemed so far away that even the snow, his sled and his skates felt unreal. He tossed and turned, finding it hard to go to sleep.

Then he remembered his friends. Would he have to fit in again, like before? How would Peter and the others greet him? *I hope they will still like me when I return*, thought Jaime.

And he began to worry.

As Jaime turned over in bed, he felt something beside him. It was the box with the conch shell. He didn't remember leaving it on his bed. In fact, he had forgotten all about it. He had even visited his great-uncle several times. Jaime had thanked him for the wood carving of the boy fishing by the river. But he had never even mentioned the shell.

Tomorrow he would visit Tío Ernesto and have a talk. "And, I'm bringing you along," he told the shell.

At sunrise the next morning as the roosters crowed, Jaime pedaled his bike up the narrow winding dirt road. A few times he stopped to rest and watched the foggy mist over the hills evaporate under the hot sun.

"Tío," said Jaime sadly when he reached his great-uncle's house. "It's soon time to go away again."

"I know," said Tío Ernesto. "I've been expecting you."

"It doesn't work anymore," he told his great-uncle and handed him the box with the shell. "It lost its magic. It used to bring me back to Montaña Verde when I was in New York City. Now it doesn't do a thing."

Tío Ernesto looked at Jaime. Then he picked up the box and told Jaime to sit, and gave him some fresh, cool lemonade.

"What are you worried about, Jaime?" asked Tío Ernesto, taking the shell out of the box. "What do you want to remember?"

"I'm afraid to go back to New York. What if I don't like it there? What if my friends there don't like me anymore?"

"Here," said Tío Ernesto and offered the shell back to Jaime. "Now try to remember."

Jaime took out the shell and placed it close to his ear. He concentrated and thought of the playground back in New York City. He remembered his friends and how much fun they'd had.

Suddenly, Jaime heard the roaring sea and felt the conch shell sparkle in his hands. Its glow grew brighter and brighter. White clouds appeared. Gleaming snowflakes fell from above.

Jaime watched with wonder as streets, buildings, sidewalks, bushes and trees all covered with snow came into sight. He felt his boots crunching the white cushiony snow underneath.

The cold snowflakes fell on his face and

turned into drops of water. Jaime inhaled the chilly wet air. Traffic and people milled all around him.

He heard his name being called. There they were! Peter, Gina, Kevin and Sheila were all waving for him to come over.

He slid and slipped alongside the children. They had a snowball fight and chased each other, tumbling onto a pile of powdery snow.

Jaime continued playing until he heard Tío Ernesto calling out to him. Then he found himself back in his great-uncle's wooden cabin.

"Jaime," said Tío Ernesto. "It seems you have remembered."

"Yes, Tío," cried Jaime. "I was there! I was in New York playing in the snow with my friends. The shell got back its magic!"

Tío Ernesto smiled. "The magic was always there."

"But I don't understand, Tío," said Jaime, somewhat confused.

"What you feel deep inside is your own real power and magic," answered Tío Ernesto. "It is one's own inner strength that makes *true* magic happen."

Then Tío Ernesto took back the shell. "You really don't even need this anymore," he said.

"Please, Tío," said Jaime and held out his hand. "Can I keep it anyway and take it back to New York?" He definitely did not want to leave without his shell.

"Of course you can," Tío Ernesto whispered, and winked as he returned the shell to Jaime. "You never know. Sometimes you might need a little help."

With pleasure, Jaime put the box back in his bike basket.

"Remember," called Tío Ernesto as he watched Jaime ride his bicycle down the narrow path, "that *true* magic is the happiness you find within yourself."

Jaime stopped when he heard the words echo down the mountainside. He turned and waved one last time toward his great-uncle, then continued on his way.

He knew that Tío Ernesto had spoken the truth because the happiness he felt inside told him so.